Panic in Pompeii

this book belong
to: _____

Panic in Pompeii

by **L. A. Peacock**
illustrated by **Nathan Hale**

Scholastic Inc.
New York Toronto London Auckland
Sydney Mexico City New Delhi Hong Kong

For Erica Dube and Christian Rose,
who love to read — L.A.F.

ISBN 978-0-545-34062-5

Copyright © 2011 by L. A. Peacock
Illustrations copyright © 2011 by Scholastic Inc.

12 11 10 9 8 7 6 5 4 3 2   12 13 14 15 16/0

Printed in the U.S.A.   40

First Scholastic printing, September 2011

Chapter 1

The Magic Trunk

Jess peeked into the dark attic.

"Do you see it?" whispered Josh.

Jess's ten-year-old twin brother held the flashlight.

"Yeah," she said. "It's still there. In the corner."

The beam of light was pointed at a large trunk. It was covered with stickers from all over the world: Greece, Egypt, China, and more. The old trunk belonged to their uncle Harry, a famous explorer and time traveler.

They hurried over to the trunk.

"Open it," said Jess. The last time they looked inside, there was nothing except some books and family photographs.

Slowly, Josh raised the lid and leaned over. He shined the flashlight around inside the trunk.

"Well," said Jess, "anything new there?"

Josh smiled. He pulled out a leather shoulder bag.

"It's heavy!" cried Josh with excitement, handing Uncle Harry's bag to Jess.

She reached in and felt a round metal object.

"It's here," she said. It was the time-compass.

"Give it to me," said Josh. He knew how to work the mysterious device. It had two hands like a clock and a third hand for direction: N, S, E, or W.

When Uncle Harry needed the kids' help, he left the time-compass in the trunk. Josh and Jess followed clues to find their uncle. In their last adventure, the time-compass had taken them to ancient Egypt.

"Maybe Uncle Harry left us a message," said Jess.

"Oh, right," said Josh. He put down the time-compass. The number marks were different than last time. The Egyptian hieroglyphs were gone. The new marks looked like more familiar letters.

He looked again. At the bottom of the trunk, Josh saw an old brown book. Uncle Harry's journal.

Josh flipped through the pages. He found his uncle's last entry.

"Roman times," said Josh. He pointed to Pompeii and Mount Vesuvius.

"Oh, great," said Jess. "Uncle Harry is in Pompeii." They had studied about Vesuvius, the volcano that had buried the ancient Roman town of Pompeii long ago.

"Cool," said Josh. *They were going on a new adventure!*

Jess emptied the leather bag.

"Look," she said. "There's more." Two coins fell out. And a strange wooden book.

Josh picked up the silver coins. One showed a man wearing a helmet. The other, a mountain. Around the edges was funny writing.

"Wow," said Josh. "Money. Old money."

Jess reached out and grabbed the wooden book.

"Hey," said Jess, "this old book must be from Pompeii." Their uncle left ancient objects in the trunk to keep them safe while he looked for their true owners.

A pointed stick slipped out of the book. The book's inside covers were coated in wax. Strange writing was scratched into the wax. There were no inside pages.

Jess looked up. Josh was staring at the old coins.

"More clues from Uncle Harry," said Jess. She traced the funny letters scratched into the wax.

Josh put the coins into the leather bag and leaned over.

"Yeah," he said. "The Roman alphabet looks a lot like ours." *Pompeii* was clear. But the letters on the right side made no sense.

"What's L-X-X-I-X?" asked Josh. Did Uncle Harry send them number clues to set the time-compass?

Jess grabbed the Book Wizard from the pocket of her sweatshirt. She read electronic books. Mysteries were her favorite. The Wizard's encyclopedia helped Jess look up all kinds of facts, too.

She pressed the Search button.

"Roman numerals," answered Jess. "We have digits like 1, 2, 3. The Romans used letters."

"Let me see," said Josh. He moved in closer.

o wizard

In Roman numerals,

I = 1 C = 100

V = 5 D = 500

X = 10 M = 1,000

L = 50

Josh grabbed a pencil and wrote LXXIX in the journal.

"The LXX must mean seventy," said Josh. "L for fifty, and two Xs for twenty." He looked puzzled.

"What does the IX at the end mean?"

Jess clicked to the next screen and read aloud:

```
o wizard
```

The value of Roman numerals never changes:

I always means 1.

X always means 10.

Add the numerals when smaller numerals follow larger numerals.

For example, XXII = 22

Subtract smaller numerals when they come before larger numerals.

For example, IL = 49

"Cool," said Josh. "Then IX means nine. And LXXIX means seventy-nine."

He wrote the year 79 in the journal. Now they could set the time-compass.

Josh put the wax book and journal into the leather bag and handed it to Jess. He reached for the time-travel device and set the hands to 79.

"Wait," said Jess. She typed a few words. The Wizard screen lit up.

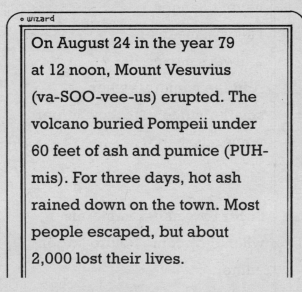

○ wizard

On August 24 in the year 79 at 12 noon, Mount Vesuvius (va-SOO-vee-us) erupted. The volcano buried Pompeii under 60 feet of ash and pumice (PUH-mis). For three days, hot ash rained down on the town. Most people escaped, but about 2,000 lost their lives.

"I have a bad feeling about this," said Jess, shaking her head. They were going to Pompeii. A city destroyed by a volcano.

"Come on, Jess," said Josh. "Uncle Harry needs our help."

Jess took a deep breath. She could hear the clicking sounds of the time-compass. The room was spinning. The walls of the attic were shaking.

She reached out and grabbed Josh's hand.

A bright light flashed.

They covered their eyes.

Suddenly, everything was quiet.

Chapter 2
The Busy Port

"Cute dress," said Jess. She looked down at her new clothes.

"I like yours, too," said Jess. Josh also was wearing a white tunic and lace-up sandals.

"Oh, man," said Josh, shaking his head. *A dress. Again.*

He tightened the belt around his waist. The early morning sunlight felt warm on his arms and legs. His jeans, T-shirt, and sneakers were gone. More magic from the time-compass.

Josh raised his hand to shelter his eyes.

A blue sea was all around them. They were on a ship. Up ahead was a busy port. A road led up to a town of large buildings and white stone houses with red tile roofs. Olive trees covered the hillside. It was a pretty seaside town.

"Pompeii," whispered Josh. He pointed to large bridges curving down the hillside. They were held up by high arches.

"What are those things?"

Jess searched the Wizard.

"Aqueducts," she answered, turning the screen toward Josh.

An aqueduct (A-kwa-dukt)
carried water from faraway
lakes to huge cisterns, or tanks.
Pipes and tunnels under the
streets delivered the water to
fountains throughout the city.

"The ancient Romans were great builders,"
said Jess. "Some of these aqueducts are still
standing."

Their ship was pulling into the harbor.

Jess put away the Wizard and handed Uncle
Harry's leather bag to Josh.

He slung the leather bag across his back.

Inside were Uncle Harry's journal, the time-compass, the silver coins, and the mysterious wax book. Now they had to find Uncle Harry.

"Look!" said Jess. She pointed to a dark mountain just behind the town. "That must be Mount Vesuvius."

Josh leaned forward over the railing. A chill ran down his back. *Was there smoke streaming from the top of Vesuvius?*

"Come on," cried Jess. She was already off the ship. Workers on the dock were busy unloading large baskets of grains and fruits. Some carried large jars of wine and oil. Others were dragging cages of wild animals. Pompeii was a busy Roman port.

Josh took a last look around. The waves were choppy. Strange. Waves but no wind. Seabirds were flying around, but they made no sound. It was unusually quiet.

"Watch out!" yelled Josh, waving at his sister below.

Jess heard a low growl and turned. A large black dog jumped out at Jess. He showed his sharp teeth and barked loudly. Just then, a large muscled man pulled back on the leash.

"Yikes!" Jess screamed. She stepped back against one of the cages.

The dog kept barking as the man led him away. He went back to his animals. But not before he gave Jess a mean look.

Josh rushed down to the dock and grabbed Jess's arm. His sister was always getting into trouble.

"Oh, man," said Josh. "That was close."

A low whimpering sound was coming from the cage behind Jess.

"Wait," said Jess. She knelt down and stared into the cage. A small brown bear was chained to the metal bars. He was barely moving in the hot sun.

Looking around, Jess reached for a clay bowl and filled it with water from a barrel. She slipped it through the bars of the cage. The bear quickly lapped up all the water.

Jess smiled at the thirsty bear.

"Hey!" shouted the giant of a man. "Get away from my bear!" The man was angry, sticking his thick, hairy arm into the cage. He pushed the bear back into the corner.

"We better get out of here," warned Josh. He pulled his sister away. But not before Jess turned and raised her fist.

"Oh, yeah!" she shouted. "You ugly bully. I'll see you later."

"Now we're in big trouble!" said Josh. He pushed Jess ahead.

They ran as fast as they could toward the city gate.

Chapter 3

The Forum

The road from the port was paved with flat stones. Jess and Josh moved with the crowd up the hillside to the opening in the city wall. The gate had two separate paths. One for carts and carriages. The other for people on foot.

Suddenly, Jess stopped. She glanced at Josh. The ground was shaking slightly.

"Did you feel that?" whispered Jess. She felt a chill up her spine and grabbed Josh's tunic.

"Listen," Josh said. Cows were moaning. Dogs were howling.

Jess looked scared.

"No birds," she said. They had stopped singing.

Josh nodded. "Just loud noises from the cows and dogs."

Other people were stopping. They felt the rumbles in the ground, too.

Then everything was quiet again. The people moved on.

"This is really weird," whispered Jess.

Josh tried to be brave. "Don't worry. Just little tremors."

They slipped through the town gate and into the busy street. The main square of Pompeii was just ahead. It was a large open space where traders set up shops. Dozens of stalls opened onto the central market.

"Oh, man," said Josh, looking around. "How are we ever going to find Uncle Harry?"

Clothing, perfumes, and silver plates were spread out on tables. Farmers were selling fruits and grains. There was much shouting as shoppers crowded around the stalls.

Next to them, a woman was buying some fresh fish. Some kids were trying on shoes. A man was stacking cages filled with live pigeons.

"Yeah," said Josh. "Just like the shopping mall at home."

"Are you nuts?" said Jess. She held her nose. Fish guts? The smells from the cooking stalls were strong.

They walked ahead and stopped in front of a large temple. Tall stone columns lined the entrance. They walked up the long staircase and sat down. Statues of gods and goddesses filled spaces along the walls.

Jess reached into her pocket for the Wizard. She searched for "Pompeii," then for the city plan. She read aloud:

The *forum*, or central market,
was just inside the city gates.
It was filled with shops and
public buildings. The Temple of
Apollo opened into the forum.
Apollo was the Greek god
of the sun, also worshipped
by the Romans. The Romans
prayed to many gods and
goddesses and celebrated
them in public holidays.

"Anything else?" asked Josh.
Jess clicked to the next screen.

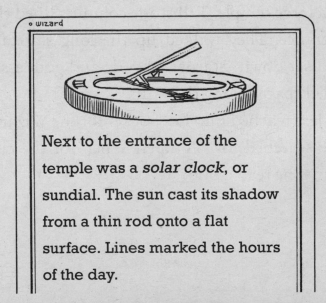

Next to the entrance of the
temple was a *solar clock*, or
sundial. The sun cast its shadow
from a thin rod onto a flat
surface. Lines marked the hours
of the day.

Jess rushed to the top of the high staircase.

"Let's check the time," said Jess, pulling Josh up behind her.

"Here," said Josh, leaning over the sundial. He pointed to the different hour marks. "The sun moves across the sky, then the shadow line changes."

Jess moved in closer. The shadow was on a Roman numeral.

"V-I-I-I," she read the letters out loud. "Eight o'clock."

Josh looked up at the morning sun. "Four more hours."

Jess nodded. Noon. That was when Vesuvius would blow its top.

Four more hours before the volcano.

Four more hours to find Uncle Harry.

Chapter 4
A Snack

"We'd better go," said Jess. The temple was getting crowded.

Josh watched people leaving gifts of food for the gods.

"I wonder where we can get breakfast," said Josh. He was hungry.

Jess smiled.

"Pizza," she said. Her favorite food.

They headed back down the stairs toward the market. The smell of fresh bread was coming from around the corner. They stopped in front of the bakery.

Brick ovens lined the back wall. The fire below was burning hot. A man was removing large flat loaves of bread. In the next stall, two women covered the breads with spicy sauces and herbs. Customers were eating standing up.

They heard a voice.

"Try the fish sauce. It's delicious."

Jess turned around. They could understand the ancient Roman language. First the zookeeper, now this boy. It was magic from the time-compass.

"Josh," she whispered. "He's speaking Latin." She pointed to the boy next to them. He was about their age. A cloth bag was strapped across his chest. It was filled with paper scrolls.

Josh nodded.

"No, thanks," he answered the boy in Latin. "I'll skip the sauce. Just plain for me." He ordered two pizzas and paid with one of Uncle Harry's coins.

Josh handed Jess one of the hot flat breads. It was dripping with olive oil and sweet herbs. He took a bite of his pizza.

"Yummy," said Josh. He wiped his mouth with the skirt of his tunic.

"Gross," complained Jess. She made a face at her brother.

The Roman boy laughed.

"Spartacus," he said, reaching across the table to shake Josh's hand.

"I'm Josh. This is my sister, Jess." They shook hands.

In front of them, some kids were playing a game. They were crouched around a circle scratched in the ground.

"What are they playing?" asked Jess.

"Knucklebones," said Spartacus. "You toss up one of the knucklebones and try to scoop up some of the others."

Jess leaned in to watch.

"And then you catch the first one before it hits the ground," added Jess. The game was like jacks, which kids played at home.

"Do you play dice?" asked Spartacus. He reached into his pocket and pulled out a coin. "I'll wager you this if you win."

Spartacus took a place around the circle.

"Oh, no," cried Jess. "I don't play. But it looks like fun."

"Why is it called knucklebones?" asked Josh. Uncle Harry's other coin was in his hand.

Their new friend looked up. "The dice are small, square bones. From a sheep's foot. The knucklebones."

Jess covered her mouth. "Now that's *really* gross."

Laughing, Josh found a place around the circle. He tossed the coin into the middle and scooped up the bones. It was his turn.

"Great," groaned Jess. Uncle Harry was missing. The volcano was ready to blow. Now Josh was playing games.

They played three rounds of knucklebones. Jess watched Josh lose the last of Uncle Harry's coins.

"Bad luck," said Spartacus, picking up his winnings.

"Take this." He handed the silver coin back to Josh. Then he took the paper scrolls out of his bag. "Help me hang these around the forum."

Jess picked up one of the scrolls.

"Gladiator games?" she said. Jess held the poster for Josh to see.

"Today," said Spartacus. "I train at the gladiator school. My grandfather's father was a famous gladiator. I'm named after him," he said proudly.

Jess looked closely at the picture. The gladiator's face looked familiar. So did the ponytail at the back of his neck.

Josh was staring, too.

It was Uncle Harry.

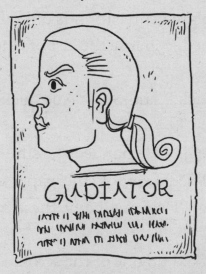

Chapter 5
The Amphitheater

Jess held the gladiator poster in her hands.

"You have to help us," she pleaded.

"That's our uncle," said Josh. "Can you take us to him?"

Spartacus gulped. He wanted to help his new friends.

"Come along," said Spartacus, turning down the street. He knew this gladiator. A stranger, but a good fighter.

Spartacus headed away from the forum. The market was behind them. They turned at the next corner and stopped. People were gathered around a public fountain, waiting

 to fill their water jars. But the pipes and cistern were empty.

"Strange," said Spartacus. "There's no water. That never happens." Shaking his head, he waved for Josh and Jess to follow.

The air was still.

"No sound," said Jess. She looked worried.

"Yeah," Josh said. It was quiet, too quiet.

Josh and Jess looked at each other, then raced after Spartacus. They were running out of time.

Up ahead, they passed wooden houses facing each side of the street. From the upper floors, some women were at the windows. They emptied jars and baskets into the street.

"Watch out!" yelled Jess, stepping to the side. Some rotten fruit and vegetables splashed in front of them.

Josh ducked.

"Whew," he sighed. An overripe tomato just missed his head.

"Follow me," shouted Spartacus, "if you don't want to get wet." Carefully, he skipped along the raised stones in the street.

Josh saw other garbage floating in the gutters along the edges. He grabbed Jess's hand. They jumped from stone to stone until they reached a wide, open space.

Jess turned on the Wizard. She searched for "Roman towns" and "sewers."

Rainwater collected in the gutters. Sewers under the streets carried the town's waste to the sea.

Aqueducts. Fountains. Sewers. The Romans were great engineers and builders.

"Look," said Josh. Up ahead was a huge building, like a football stadium. It was three stories high, almost a full circle. Tall stone arches held up the rows of seats.

"That's the amphitheater," said Spartacus. "More than twenty thousand people can watch the games."

In front of them was the main entrance. Several soldiers stood on each side. Hundreds of people were lined up for the afternoon games.

"Over here," whispered Spartacus. Next to him was a side door. The twins followed him into a long tunnel beneath the seats. It opened onto a wide arena. The floor was covered with sand.

Jess stepped out. She looked up and shielded her eyes from the hot sun.

"Almost noon," said Jess. The sun was high in the sky.

Josh glanced up. In the distance, Vesuvius looked dark and scary. More white smoke streamed from the top of the mountain. Below, the ground was shaking.

Jess felt the deep rumbles through her thin sandals. So did Josh and Spartacus.

"Don't worry," said Spartacus. "It does that a lot here. We citizens of Pompeii are used to these little tremors. The mountain is asleep."

Jess knew better. *This mountain is waking up!*

"It won't be long," she whispered into Josh's ear.

Joss nodded. They had to find Uncle Harry and get out of Pompeii.

Just then, a lion roared. Jess turned and saw a group of cages along the wall next to them. Behind the lion cages, some monkeys were jumping wildly. In the next cage, she spotted the small brown bear from the docks.

Just near the last cage stood the giant zookeeper. And his barking dog.

Chapter 6
The Plan

Jess and Josh stepped back into the tunnel.

"Yikes," said Jess. "That was close."

The mean zookeeper opened the cage. He tied a rope around the bear's neck. They took their place behind the elephant. Other men were moving the lion cages into a straight line behind them.

Josh grabbed Jess's hand. They walked slowly after Spartacus, along the wall, away from the cages.

Suddenly, they dashed toward the other side of the arena. Jess turned to take a last look at the zookeeper. He looked straight at Jess and scowled.

"People like the wild animals," said Spartacus. "The animal hunts are almost as popular as the gladiator contests."

Jess shook her head.

"No," she said. "It's wrong." *How could she help the poor beasts?*

"Hurry." Josh pulled Jess away.

Spartacus pointed to places on the arena floor where the sand was darker.

"Look there," he said. "Hidden beneath the sand floor are tunnels with trapdoors. The doors open to let animals and gladiators come out from below."

"Yeah," said Josh. "A surprise for the fighters." *Could these hidden passages help them?*

Just then a trumpet sounded.

A parade entered the arena. The musicians came first, led by a man playing a large curved horn. Then the soldiers marched. The animals came next. The zookeeper held the rope tied to

the brown bear. Dancers and jugglers followed.
The gladiators came last.

Jess leaned in to get a better look.

A line of tall men marched across the arena.
Their heads were covered with bronze helmets.
They carried heavy shields, swords, and metal
nets. Leather straps crossed their wide muscled
chests.

"Do you see Uncle Harry?" asked Josh.

Jess shook her head.

Suddenly, the crowd began to shout wildly. All heads turned as a single gladiator ran into the arena.

Spartacus pointed to the man.

"That's him," he said. "The man on the poster. They call him 'The Stranger.'"

The people stood in their seats. They cheered loudly and stamped their feet.

Jess felt the Wizard in her pocket, pulled it out, and typed in some words.

"Look," she said, showing the screen to Josh.

○ Wizard

Gladiators were trained fighters. They battled other gladiators and wild animals in amphitheaters. Some gladiators were slaves. Others got paid for fighting.

Jess and Josh glanced at each other.

Uncle Harry. Here. In the arena.

They stared at the last gladiator.

"We have to help him," cried Jess. She turned to Spartacus.

"We need a plan," she said. "To save our uncle."

"An escape plan," said Josh.

Spartacus nodded. He knew this gladiator. A stranger, but a good man.

"This way," he said. Soon they were back in the tunnels.

"Watch your head," warned Spartacus. They raced through several passageways crossing below the arena.

"Whew!" said Jess, ducking from the spiderwebs. Rats crawled near her feet. It was dark and dirty belowground.

Jess rested against a large post. Some light was coming from the ceiling overhead.

Spartacus stopped. He started to turn a large metal wheel. Attached were heavy ropes leading from an elevator platform to the trapdoor above.

"Jess," said Spartacus. "Stand on the elevator. Josh can pull you up. Your uncle should be about here."

A beam of light fell through the crack of the trapdoor. Jess looked up. She was scared.

"Don't be chicken," said Josh.

Jess tried to smile. "Okay," she said in a quiet voice. She wasn't so sure about this plan.

Slowly she pulled herself up onto the elevator platform.

"Brave girl," whispered Spartacus. He turned and ran down another tunnel.

"Where are you going?" shouted Josh.

"To the beasts," cried Spartacus. "A big cat on the loose will make the crowd go wild."

Josh nodded. Good thinking.

"Listen for the horns and shouting," said Spartacus. "People will cheer for the animals. Then Jess can pull your uncle away."

Spartacus disappeared into the dark tunnel.

Josh took the wheel of the elevator.

"Okay," Jess said. "I'm ready."

They waited. In a few minutes, cries came from the crowd. They heard loud roars. Horns were blowing. People were running above them.

The beasts had escaped into the arena.

They heard more loud roars. Gladiators were chasing the big cats.

Josh turned the wheel. The elevator moved up slowly.

Jess crouched down. The trapdoor opened above.

She peeked into the arena.

Suddenly, two strong arms lifted her up into the air.

Chapter 7
The Escape

"Uncle Harry!" cried Jess.

Her uncle pulled off his helmet and dropped his shield. He held her tight.

"Awesome," he said and grinned. "Where did you come from? And where's your brother?"

A shout came from below.

"Hurry, let's go!" cried Josh.

Josh started to lower the elevator. Uncle Harry held on to Jess and jumped onto the elevator platform.

When they reached the tunnel floor, Josh hugged his uncle.

"Here," said Josh, handing over the leather bag.

Uncle Harry glanced inside. The time-compass, journal, and wax book were safe.

"Good job," he said proudly. The kids had saved him again.

They heard sounds from the tunnel.

Spartacus was back. He waved for them to follow.

"Spartacus!" shouted Uncle Harry. He was smiling. The boy from the training school was helping them escape.

"This way," said Spartacus. He pointed to a path through the dark tunnel.

They raced through the underground maze. Finally there was light. A gate was open up ahead.

"Wait," said Jess. "We'll be back."

She grabbed Spartacus's hand. They turned and disappeared back down the tunnel.

"Where are you going?" shouted Josh.

Jess looked back. "The cages," she cried. "To free the bear."

Josh kept shaking his head. *Jess is nuts. She is going to get into trouble.*

A hand was on his shoulder.

"Don't worry," said Uncle Harry. "Everything will be fine. Spartacus knows the way. She's safe with him."

"Sit," said his uncle.

Josh slumped down and sat on the dusty ground. Uncle Harry sat down beside him.

"So tell me," asked Josh, "were you really a gladiator?"

Uncle Harry laughed. "No, not really. I told them I was a fighter. A champion from Rome."

"But weren't you scared?" wondered Josh. "The wild animals. The lions. The other gladiators."

His uncle shrugged. "The games are in the

afternoon. Remember. And today is August twenty-fourth."

Josh looked up. Noon. There would be panic in Pompeii soon.

"Right," he said. "No games today."

Uncle Harry pulled the wax book from the leather bag. He opened it wide. The letters LXXIX were scratched into the wax.

"The year seventy-nine," said Josh. "That's how we set the time-compass."

Uncle Harry nodded. He had left the book in the old trunk to keep it safe.

"I have to return this book," said Uncle Harry.

Josh knew about his uncle's dangerous missions. He was a famous explorer and time traveler. He found objects lost in time and returned them to their true owners.

"Who does *that* belong to?" asked Josh, pointing to the wax book.

Uncle Harry turned the ancient book over in his hand. "A young lawyer."

It was almost noon.

Uncle Harry wrote some notes in his journal.

The ground began to shake again. More than before.

"Oh, man," said Josh. "This is it. The eruption."

He turned to Uncle Harry.

"Where's Jess?" Josh whispered.

More tremors.

They stood for a moment and listened.

The earth below was moving with large rumbles.

A giant blast pierced the still air.

"Oh, no," said Josh.

Vesuvius.

Chapter 8

The Big Blast

The earth moved with a tremendous jolt. The air was shaking with thunder. All eyes in the amphitheater were on the giant umbrella cloud of black dirt and white ash above Vesuvius. Bolts of lightning cut through the dark sky.

Uncle Harry and Josh raced to the tunnel entrance and looked out.

"What's happening?" cried Josh. Cracks split the walls above the arches. Everything was falling around them.

Uncle Harry pointed to Vesuvius. The top of the mountain had blown off.

"Erupted," he said. Uncle Harry pulled his

leather bag tight across his chest. "We'd better find your sister," he said, "and get out of here."

A giant cloud was advancing down the hillside toward the town. It was black and huge. In a short time, the sky was covered by a dark curtain of volcanic dust.

The people around them screamed in horror. They knocked each other over as they rushed through the arena gates. Some people were hit by large stones falling from the split columns.

Josh heard sounds from the tunnel. Running feet. A dog barking.

"Did you hear that?" asked Josh, glancing back behind his shoulder.

Two small figures appeared. They were covered in dirt.

"You okay?" asked Uncle Harry. He wiped the dirt from their clothes and hair.

Spartacus nodded. Jess was too out of breath to speak.

"We opened the cages," said Spartacus with

excitement. "The bear. The monkeys. They're all free."

"Then came the blast," added Jess. "It was awful."

Jess looked behind her. Heavy footsteps. The barking was louder.

"More trouble," she said. "The zookeeper is chasing us. He saw us at the cages."

The tremors had stopped.

Quickly, Uncle Harry pushed the kids toward the entrance.

"Okay, let's go," he yelled above the screams of the crowd. Frightened people filled the streets. They were fleeing the city as fast as they could.

All around them, people were coughing and covering their mouths. The air was thick with ash. The dust in the air made it hard to breathe. Snowlike powder was covering the streets. Soon there were several inches of the white stuff on the ground.

"Watch out," yelled Spartacus. He shuffled carefully through the white powder. The streets below were torn up by the tremors.

Clay tiles were falling from rooftops. Buildings on both sides of the streets were cracked, shifting back and forth.

The kids raced through the broken streets after Uncle Harry. They had just passed the forum.

Many people were knocked down by the falling buildings. Screaming, they fell over their bundles of clothes and household things. Some people pulled on donkeys. Baskets on the donkeys' backs were filled with belongings. The animals, too, were screeching loudly.

Most of the fleeing people were headed to the South Gate. Toward the harbor.

Uncle Harry was leading them north, on a street up the hill.

"Where are we going?" asked Josh. He looked up at the volcano.

Jess was confused, too. *Shouldn't they be going in the other direction? Away from the volcano?*

Uncle Harry turned to Spartacus.

"Do you know the House of Vetti?" he asked. "We need to go there."

Spartacus nodded. The villa was famous in Pompeii. It belonged to an important family.

"Follow me," he said. He took a street to the left. Then another up the hill. A fountain was on the corner. Some water was dripping from the pipe.

"There's water here!" shouted Uncle Harry, staring at the fountain. "Where is it coming from?"

Spartacus pointed to the top of the hill. "The Public Baths are near the North Gate. Close to the town's biggest aqueduct."

After several more streets, they rounded the corner and came to a large house. A picture of a fierce dog covered the floor of the entrance.

"Is that it?" asked Josh.

Uncle Harry shook his head.

Jess reached for the Wizard. The screen lit up. She typed some words.

CAVE CANEM

This mosaic from Pompeii warned visitors to "beware of the dog."

"*Cave canem* — beware of the dog," said Jess.

"It's a mosaic," said Uncle Harry. "The picture is made of small pieces of colored stones."

"Dogs," said Jess, shaking her head. "Big dogs. Angry dogs." She was thinking of the dog from the dock.

"The dogs protect the houses," said Spartacus. "People are afraid of thieves."

"Come," he said, taking Jess's hand.

Spartacus pointed to the house next door. "The zookeeper lives there."

Jess looked at Josh.

"Oh, no!" she cried. "Do you think *he's* here?"

Josh shook his head. Jess was still afraid of that mean zookeeper.

"Don't be silly," he said. "He's probably at the South Gate by now."

Jess glanced down the street. She wasn't so sure.

Spartacus led them to another street. It was hard to see. The shower of ash from the volcano was getting heavier. Light stones were now mixed with the ash.

"Oh, man," yelled Josh, shielding his head. "It's raining rocks now!"

The white stones clattered on the street.

With each step, they sank deeper into the volcanic ash.

"The house you want is up ahead!" shouted Spartacus. "The House of Vetti."

Uncle Harry peeked in.

"Awesome," he said. The villa looked empty.

He tried the latch. The doors were unlocked.

There was more pounding on the roof.

"Get inside," said Uncle Harry, pushing the kids toward the open doors.

Away from the raining rocks.

Chapter 9

The Villa

"Look at this," said Jess, turning around. The walls were filled with beautiful paintings. There were pictures of the family, Roman gods, and hunting scenes. Statues lined the walls.

"More mosaics." Josh pointed to the colorful tiles on the floor.

"This one has an octopus," she said, tracing the pattern of tiny tiles.

"Yeah," said Josh, "and small fish all around it."

They were in a large open hall with a hole in the ceiling. A pool was in the middle of the room just below.

"Hey," said Jess. "They have a swimming pool."

Spartacus laughed. "No," he said. "The pool catches the rainwater. For drinking. This is the best part of the house."

Uncle Harry left with Spartacus to check the other rooms.

"Cool," said Josh. "Look at the statues. Roman gods. To protect the house."

Jess sat on the edge of the little pool. She turned on the Wizard and searched for "Roman houses" and read aloud:

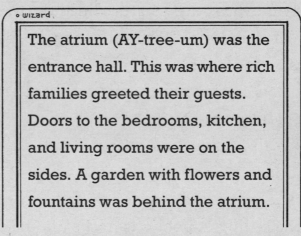

The atrium (AY-tree-um) was the entrance hall. This was where rich families greeted their guests. Doors to the bedrooms, kitchen, and living rooms were on the sides. A garden with flowers and fountains was behind the atrium.

Their uncle returned.

"The owners are gone," said Uncle Harry. He

stretched out his legs next to Jess. The leather bag was on his lap.

Spartacus rushed into the atrium from the other side. "There's food on the tables in there."

"Yeah," said Jess. "I bet the owners left with the first tremors."

Uncle Harry pulled out the wax book from his bag.

"What's that book?" asked Spartacus. "Is it yours?"

Uncle Harry shook his head. He turned the ancient book in his hand. "It belongs to a young lawyer."

He got up slowly. "Time to find its owners. Their house is near here."

"I'll go with you," said Spartacus. "I can help." He raced to the doorway and lit a torch. It was as dark as night outside.

Uncle Harry turned to Jess and Josh.

"Wait here," he said. "Find us some food."

He looked up at the hole in the ceiling. The

sky was dark from the falling ash. The rocks were still raining down from the volcano. They needed to get to the South Gate soon.

"Watch this," he said handing the leather bag to Josh.

"Sure," said Josh.

The door closed behind them.

Jess felt tired. And hungry.

"Come on," she said. "Let's find the dining room."

They stepped into a large room. Three

couches were next to each other. Each couch faced a side of a low square table in the center. On the open side, servers could bring and remove the dishes.

The table was filled with food.

"Wow," said Josh. "Grapes. Meat. Eggs. Honey cakes." Everything looked fresh.

"They left in a hurry," said Jess. Noon, when the volcano erupted.

"More for us," said Josh. He moved some pillows and lay down on one of the fancy

couches. Josh grabbed a bunch of grapes and started to eat.

"Hey," yelled Jess. "Leave some for the rest of us."

Josh filled the leather bag with bread, cheese, and fruit. Uncle Harry and Spartacus would be hungry, too.

Jess pulled the Wizard from her pocket.

"I wonder who owns that wax book," said Jess. She typed some words and searched.

This portrait shows a lawyer and his wife with a wax book. Two leaves of the book fold together to protect the writing. The man is holding a scroll.

Jess held up the screen.

"I guess books with pages were invented later," said Josh.

Jess clicked and searched some more:

> o wizard
>
> Romans wrote by scratching on panels of wood coated with wax. They used a metal pen called a *stylus*. They scraped off old writing with the flat end of the stylus and wrote again on the same tablet.

Just then they heard a loud rumbling sound.

"What's happening?" said Josh, looking up. The ceiling was starting to sag. Pieces of plaster were falling on their heads.

"Duck!" he yelled, shielding his head from the falling ceiling.

Jess looked down. The ground was shaking, too. Small cracks ran along the mosaic floor.

Then it was quiet again.

"You okay?" asked Josh. He coughed from the dust in the air.

Jess nodded. She shook the plaster from her tunic. Chunks of ceiling dotted the floor.

Suddenly, the main door to the villa burst open. Uncle Harry raced through the atrium.

"Are you okay?" he asked.

Jess and Josh nodded.

Uncle Harry glanced at the cracks in the ceiling.

"Time to get out of here," he shouted.

"Before the roof caves in."

Chapter 10

The Public Baths

Outside, the ground was peaceful again. The shaking was over.

Spartacus peeked out the open door and glanced up. A shower of rocks was pounding on the roof. The roof tiles were coming loose and falling.

They stepped into the street.

"Wait!" cried Uncle Harry, and everyone stopped. "The rocks are coming down harder now."

Up and down the street, people were stumbling out of houses. They had pillows on their heads. Strips of cloth held them in place.

Uncle Harry turned. He pulled Josh and Jess back inside. Spartacus followed.

"Quick," he said. "Grab the pillows from the couches." With his knife, Uncle Harry cut long strips of cloth from his tunic.

He held the pillow on Josh's head and tied it on tight.

"Can I help?" asked Jess. She leaned over and made a knot under his chin.

In a few minutes, they each had pillows around their heads.

Under a shower of rocks, they ran from the villa. Houses were falling. Roofs were caving in all around.

People on the street tried to step over the rubble. They were moving as fast as they could. Some were coughing from the dust. Others were crying and shouting.

Jess stopped. She was stuck in the middle of the street.

"I can't walk," cried Jess. "The stones are too deep." She looked down at her legs. Her knees were buried in the rocks.

"Grab my hand," said Josh. He tried to pull her up.

Jess stood for a few seconds. Soon she was sliding back and forth over the rocks. Then she fell again.

"No way," she said, shaking her head.

Uncle Harry looked up at the volcano in the distance. Lightning appeared above the mountain peak. Fires were starting on the hillside. Soon walls of fire would hit the town.

"We need to find another way," he said. "The streets are too dangerous."

"And too slow," said Josh.

They needed a new escape. Not the streets. Uncle Harry scratched his chin.

Up ahead he saw another fountain. Pompeii had more than twenty. The water was flowing.

This fountain was closer to the town water supply.

Suddenly, Uncle Harry had an idea. He turned to Spartacus.

"The Public Baths. The big one," he said. "It's near here, right?"

Spartacus nodded. He pointed to the path on the right.

"That way," he said. "That street goes to the North Gate. It's near the main aqueduct into Pompeii. The Public Baths are just inside the gate."

Uncle Harry scooped Jess into his arms. He waved for the others to follow. Carefully the boys scrambled over the rocks.

Slowly they walked through the rubble of fallen houses and volcanic rocks. They stopped when they reached a large building. It was as big as the temple near the forum. Large stone columns held up the arched entrance. In the middle of the roof was a big dome.

It was the Public Baths.

"It looks safe," said Uncle Harry. He gazed at the thick walls. "Not much damage from the tremors."

He put Jess down on the top step.

"This is a pretty place," said Jess. Painted statues and large fountains were in front.

Spartacus pushed open the heavy doors.

Josh poked his head inside.

"Hello!" he shouted. "Anybody here?"

His voice echoed. The baths were empty.

They walked through the first hall and the locker rooms. Colorful mosaics and paintings covered the floors and walls. Library rooms filled with scrolls and reading tables were on one side. A large kitchen with dining couches were on the other side.

"This is a fancy place," said Josh.

Spartacus nodded. "Everybody comes here.

To read. To eat lunch. To enjoy a swim and bath."

The next hall led into a huge room with a high ceiling. It was lined with stone columns. The dome ceiling was decorated with beautiful paintings.

"Looks like a giant ice-cream cone," said Josh, glancing up.

Jess shook her head. Her brother was always thinking about food!

"The pools are here," said Jess, running ahead. She dipped her hand in the water of the smaller pool.

"Brrr!" she said. "This pool is cold."

"And this one is hot!" said Josh. He tested the water of the large pool in the center of the room.

Spartacus nodded. "It's heated from below. First we steam ourselves in the hot water. Then dip into the cold pool."

"Where's the soap?" asked Josh.

Jess turned on the Wizard and typed in R-O-M-A-N B-A-T-H:

The Romans rubbed their skin with olive oil. Then they used a metal tool called a *strigil* to scrape off the oil and dirt.

"No soap," said Jess, looking around. She picked up a strigil next to the hot pool. "Just this funny thing."

Uncle Harry glanced back at Spartacus.

"Show me the furnace room," he said.

Spartacus stepped into the next room. The hottest room of all. Its fires were still burning.

The furnace boiled water for the baths. Pipes under the floors carried the heated water to the hot pools. The ancient Romans were skilled engineers.

Uncle Harry crawled along the biggest pipe. It carried the water into the Public Baths from the aqueduct. Then it led from the furnace to a door in the wall.

He pushed the door open. The pipe bent down into a water pump outside the door. It continued along the ground.

Uncle Harry waved to the kids.

"Stay close behind me," said their uncle. Back and forth, he followed the pipe. Part of the pipe was covered with volcanic ash and rocks. They were getting close to the North Gate.

Finally he stopped and knelt down. He pushed aside the ash and stones and found a narrow triangle of wood. It was set into the ground, almost hidden. A trapdoor.

Uncle Harry moved the last stones aside.

Spartacus pulled the handle. "Got it," he said, raising the wooden door.

"Got what?" asked Jess. Josh looked puzzled, too.

Josh and Jess moved to the edge of the open trapdoor and looked down. It was dark. A rusty metal ladder led into a deep tunnel.

Uncle Harry turned and smiled.

"Who's going first?" he asked.

Chapter 11

The Water Slide

Up on the hill, the top of the volcano was bursting with zigzagging lightning. Balls of fire rolled through the olive groves. Hundreds of fires were burning on the hillside.

"What's that awful smell?" asked Josh.

Jess crinkled her nose. "It's like rotten eggs."

Uncle Harry sniffed the air. "Sulfur," he said. They had to hurry. Soon the winds would carry a cloud of hot poison gas into the town.

Spartacus picked up a small stone. He tossed it into the deep tunnel below the trapdoor. They heard a splash. There was water below.

"What is this place?" asked Jess.

"It's called the Castellum Aquae," answered

Spartacus. He pointed to the large aqueduct just outside the North Gate.

Uncle Harry nodded. "It's a reservoir. The aqueduct carries the water into a large tank. It collects there," he explained.

"Then three big pipes carry the water into Pompeii," added Spartacus.

Josh glanced back at the water pump at the Public Baths. There was a network of pipes and fountains through all the streets of Pompeii.

He smiled. Uncle Harry had a plan to escape the volcano. Through the underground water pipes and tunnels.

"I'm first," said Josh. He stepped into the tunnel. He grabbed the top rung of the ladder and climbed down.

"Careful, Josh." His uncle's voice echoed in the dark hole.

Josh took a deep breath. He looked down. Only a few more steps. Then he jumped.

He felt the hard stone floor. Josh was up to his waist in the water.

"Oh, man," he said in a loud voice. "There's water, but it's not deep." He looked up the ladder.

Three dark shadows. They were all coming down. Jess, then Spartacus. Last was Uncle Harry.

They splashed into the water next to Josh.

"Everyone okay?" asked Uncle Harry. Three small heads nodded.

Uncle Harry walked slowly to the south side. Water splashed at his feet. His hands were against the wall. Finally he found the metal grille.

"Over here," said their uncle. He lifted away the screen. A tunnel was behind it.

One by one, Uncle Harry pushed the kids into the tunnel. The water was still below their waists.

"Move!" he shouted. "As fast as you can."

They kept walking. Down one tunnel, then another. Around one corner, then the next. The streets were above them. They were headed toward the South Gate. Under the town.

Just then a loud rumble shook the ground. Jess covered her face. Josh and Spartacus fell to their knees.

Uncle Harry stumbled over and pulled the three kids into his arms.

"Hold your breath!" he yelled and jumped into the water.

Waves of the smelly gas filled the tunnel. A wind of hot poisonous air passed over their heads. Above, in the streets, a glowing cloud of fire and ash rolled over the town. In less than a minute, the ash cooled and turned hard. Pompeii became a city frozen in time.

Another blast from the volcano shook the ground.

The water in the tunnel started to swell. A big wave caught them. Faster and faster they raced down through the flooded passageways. They rounded one corner, then another.

Finally they stopped.

Uncle Harry's head appeared first. Their uncle took a deep breath of air and stood up slowly.

"Jess, Jess!" groaned Josh. He coughed loudly. His sister slid from Uncle Harry's arms.

"Oh, my head," she cried. A bump was on her forehead.

Spartacus started to stand. He was dizzy from the wild ride.

"Cool," said Josh. *Just like the water slide at the adventure park.*

"Awesome!" said Uncle Harry. He checked the kids.

"Nothing broken," he said. "Let's go." He guided them toward the end of the tunnel.

They stepped outside. The harbor was below. The roads were filled with donkey carts and people. They were moving away from the town. Their clothes were torn, and their faces and arms were covered with white ash. The

South Gate and Vesuvius were behind them.

"Look at the mountain," said Josh. It was still burning with ash and hot rocks.

"It looks different," said Jess. "Smaller and flat on top."

"Yeah," said Spartacus. "Like someone took a big bite out of it."

Uncle Harry pulled the leather bag off his shoulder. He turned to Spartacus and gave him a silver coin.

"Take this," he said. "Can you get us seats on a wagon?"

Spartacus nodded. Then he ran down the hill toward the road.

Jess and Josh watched their friend. They waved good-bye. They knew they wouldn't see him again. Uncle Harry was holding the time-compass. He was sending them back.

"I'll take Spartacus home," said Uncle Harry. "His grandfather's farm is in the next town."

"Please, Uncle Harry," pleaded Jess. She wanted to stay.

"Can't we go with you?" asked Josh. It was too soon to end their adventure.

Uncle Harry pushed them gently behind a stone column.

He was shaking his head.

"Too dangerous," he said. "Pompeii is destroyed."

Josh looked up at the burning mountain. His uncle was right. Soon the city would be buried completely in ash.

Jess gave Uncle Harry a last hug.

"Will we see you again?" she whispered.

Uncle Harry took Jess and Josh into his arms.

"You bet," he said, handing Josh his leather journal. Their uncle left it in the trunk in the attic to keep it safe.

"Did you leave us new clues?" asked Josh.

Uncle Harry laughed. "Maybe."

He turned the hands of the time-compass.

"Ready?" he asked. They heard the familiar clicking sounds.

The twins nodded. Josh grabbed Jess's hand.

"I wish we could stay!" cried Jess.

Her words were lost in the howling wind.

The ground was spinning all around them.

A light blazed across the sky.

Everything stood still.

In a flash, they were back in the attic.

Chapter 12

Home, Sweet Home

Jess opened her eyes slowly. The old trunk was still in the corner, but her Roman clothes were gone. Josh was wearing his jeans and sneakers, too. He stood by the attic window.

"Glad to be home again?" she asked.

"Yeah," he said. "Everything is the same." He gazed at the quiet street below. Bright red and orange leaves covered the oak trees in the front yard. It was late afternoon. About the same time when they had left. More magic from the time-compass.

Josh turned and gave his sister a long look. "Are you all right?"

Jess nodded. "It was scary." The burning volcano. The shower of rocks. The cracked streets. The falling buildings.

She reached into her pocket and pulled out the Wizard.

P-O-M-P-E-I-I, she typed, then read aloud:

Eyewitness Report

A seventeen-year-old boy named Pliny (PLI-nee) the Younger wrote about what he saw from the other side of Pompeii's bay. He reported that the top of Vesuvius blew off. The town was buried in ash like snow. He saw winds of fire sweeping down the mountain.

"There's more," said Jess.

In the 1860s, archaeologists began digging out a large part of the buried city. About 2,000 people had died in the firestorm of poison gas. Hard ash covered their bodies. Over time, the bodies rotted, leaving empty spaces. The scientists poured plaster into these spaces and made statues of the buried people.

"Wow," said Josh. He leaned over Jess's shoulder.

Jess clicked to the next screen. The plaster casts showed the victims at Pompeii. Beggars. Soldiers. Families. Some people tried to cover their mouths from the ash dust. Most lay on the ground. They were crushed by the falling stones and buildings.

"Gross," she said. "Like the Egyptian mummies. But no bodies. Just the shapes they left behind."

"Oh, man," said Josh. "I'm glad we got out of Pompeii in time."

"Look at this!" she said with a groan.

○ Wizard

This shape in plaster shows a watchdog on a chain. The dog was tied up and was unable to escape.

Jess glanced at her brother.

"No," she said in a quiet voice. "It can't be . . ."

". . . the zookeeper's dog? No way," said Josh, shaking his head. His sister had a big imagination.

"Forget about it," he said. Josh looked down. Uncle Harry's journal was still in his hand. He flipped through the pages.

"Anything new?" asked Jess. Sometimes their uncle left clues about their next adventure.

"Ancient Greece," said Josh. He stared at the last page in the journal.

Jess moved in closer.

"No," she said. "I bet Uncle Harry's going to Troy." She put her finger on the new map. "Over here, where Turkey is today."

"Oh, man," said Josh with excitement. "The Trojan War."

"More trouble," said Jess, shaking her head. She remembered the story about the huge wooden horse. All the Greek king's soldiers were hidden inside.

Josh closed the journal and put it into the old trunk. The Roman coin was in his pocket. He slipped it next to Uncle Harry's book.

Their time travels with their uncle were their secret. Their parents didn't know.

The house was quiet.

"Come on," said Jess. "Mom and Dad will be home anytime."

Josh nodded. He lowered the lid of the trunk and headed for the stairs.

Without a sound, they left the attic.